First published in Great Britain in 2003 by Brimax™,
A division of Autumn Publishing Limited
Appledram Barns, Chichester PO20 7EQ

Mc Graw Hill Children's Publishing

This edition published in the United States of America in 2003 by
Gingham Dog Press
an imprint of McGraw-Hill Children's Publishing,
a Division of The McGraw-Hill Companies
8787 Orion Place
Columbus, Ohio 43240-4027

www.MHkids.com

Library of Congress Cataloging-in-Publication Data is on file with the publisher.

Printed in China.

ISBN 1-57768-492-3

1 2 3 4 5 6 7 8 9 10 BRI 09 08 07 06 05 04 03

The Little Red Hen

Retold by
John Escott

Illustrated by
Annie West

Columbus, Ohio

Deep in a valley, among rolling green hills and under a big, wide sky, there stood a farm. And on this farm, there was a little red hen. She lived in a little brown hen-house with her five tiny chicks.

A fat pink pig, a black-tailed sheepdog, and a tall gray goose also lived on the farm.

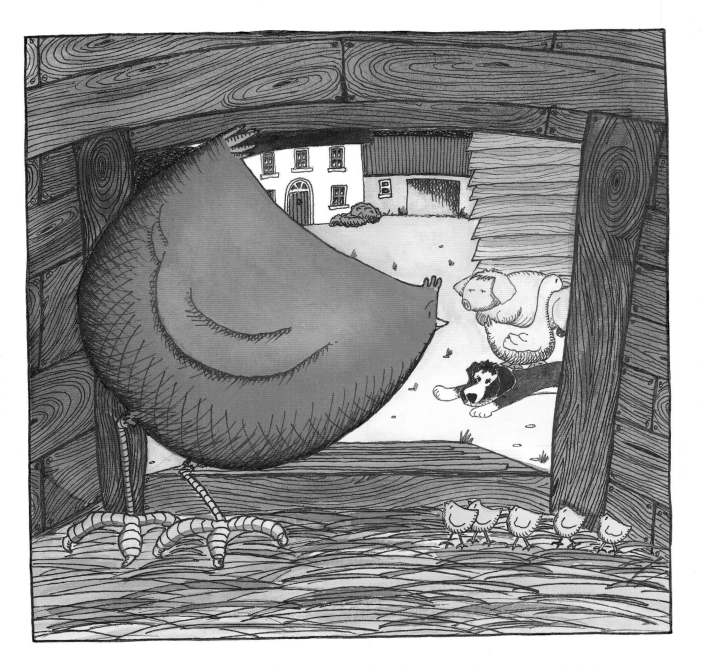

The little red hen worked hard looking after her chicks and keeping the little brown hen-house neat and tidy. But the fat pink pig, the black-tailed sheepdog, and the tall gray goose were very lazy.

How lazy, you ask?

Well, let me tell you...

One day, the little red hen was walking with her chicks when she spotted some grains of wheat on the ground. She thought for a moment or two, then carefully gathered up the grains and took them back to the farm.

"What have you there?" asked the fat pink pig.

"Some grains of wheat," replied the little red hen.
"Who will help me plant them?"

"Not I," said the fat pink pig.

"Not I," said the black-tailed sheepdog.

"Not I," said the tall gray goose.

"Then I shall plant them myself," said the little red hen.
And she did.

All through the summer, the sun shined and the rain gently fell, helping the wheat spring up from the earth, tall and golden. Soon it was ready to cut.

"Who will help me cut my wheat?" asked the little red hen.

"Not I," said the fat pink pig.

"Not I," said the black-tailed sheepdog.

"Not I," said the tall gray goose.

"Then I shall cut it myself," said the little red hen. And she did.

Now the wheat was ready to be ground into flour.

"Who will help me take it to the mill?" asked the little red hen.

"Not I," said the fat pink pig.

"Not I," said the black-tailed sheepdog.

"Not I," said the tall gray goose.

"Then I shall take it myself," said the little red hen.
And she did.

The mill was high on a hill. Up, up, up went the little red
hen until she reached the very top. And there stood a big
yellow windmill with a big green door.

"What can I do for you, little red hen?" asked the miller.

"Can you grind my wheat into flour, please?" asked the little red hen.

The miller smiled. "Of course I can," he said.
And he did.

"Thank you," said the little red hen when the miller was finished.

The miller watched as the little red hen went down, down, down the hill, pulling the heavy sack of flour behind her.

Back at the farmyard, she went to find the other animals.
"Who will help me carry this bag of flour to the baker's?"
asked the little red hen.

"Not I," said the fat pink pig.
"Not I," said the black-tailed sheepdog.
"Not I," said the tall gray goose.

"Then I will carry it myself," said the little red hen.
And she did.

The little red hen carried the heavy bag of flour into
the village. She went straight to the baker's shop.

"What can I do for you, little red hen?" asked the baker.
"Can you bake my flour into bread?" asked the little
red hen, waddling over to the counter.

The baker smiled. "Of course I can," he said.
And he did.

The baker mixed the flour into dough. Then he baked it into a warm, round loaf that smelled delicious!

"Thank you," said the little red hen when the baker had finished his work.

Then she hurried back to the farm, carefully carrying the bread.

The sweet smell of the bread filled the whole hen-house.
"We are very hungry!" said the baby chicks.

Soon the delicious aroma of bread drifted out into the farmyard.

"What's that wonderful smell?" said the fat pink pig.

"It smells like..." began the black-tailed sheepdog.

"...freshly baked bread!" finished the tall gray goose.

The three of them hurried to the little brown hen-house.

"Little red hen!" they called. "What do you have that smells so good?"

"It's my loaf of bread," replied the little red hen. "Now, who will help me eat it?"

"I will!" said the fat pink pig.

"I will!" said the black-tailed sheepdog.

"I will!" said the tall gray goose.

The little red hen slowly shook her head from side to side.

"Well, let me see," said the little red hen. "Did you help me plant and cut the wheat?"

"Er... no," said the fat pink pig, his face pinker than ever.

"Did you help me take it to the mill to be ground into flour?" asked the little red hen.

"Er... no," said the black-tailed sheepdog, his black tail drooping.

"And did you help me carry the bag of flour to the baker's to be baked into bread?" asked the little red hen.

"Er... no," said the tall gray goose, suddenly not looking so tall.

"Then you will not help me eat my bread," said the little red hen. "My chicks and I will eat it ourselves!"

And that is exactly what they did.